HEATHER, THE TOTALITY

HEATHER, THE TOTALITY

MATTHEW WEINER

CANONGATE

Published in Great Britain in 2017 by Canongate Books Ltd,
14 High Street, Edinburgh EH1 1TE

www.canongate.co.uk

1

Published in the United States by Little, Brown and Company,
Hachette Book Group, 1290 Avenue of the Americas, New York, NY 10104

British Library Cataloguing-in-Publication Data
A catalogue record for this book is available on
request from the British Library

ISBN 978 1 78689 063 4

Printed and bound in Great Britain by Clays Ltd, St Ives plc.

For Linda

ONE

MARK AND KAREN BREAKSTONE got married a little late in life. Karen was nearly 40 and had given up on finding someone as good as her father and had begun to become bitter about the seven-year relationship she'd had after college with her former Art teacher. In fact, when she was set up with Mark, she nearly turned the date down because Mark's only prominent quality was his potential to be rich. Her friend, long married and on her third pregnancy, mentioned no other qualities. Karen's married friends seemed to be obsessed with the fact that they had never considered money's importance in their relationships, having gotten married so young. Now, deeper in life they were distracted by it, sleepless as they debated their long-term security. Karen still wanted someone handsome. She felt it would be an unbearable compromise to stare at an ugly face every day and worry about her future children's orthodontia.

But no one had actually met Mark. The women knew he had a good job and wasn't from Manhattan and Karen could ask someone's husband who knew Mark, but there really wasn't time for anyone to investigate in the days before email or texting. Mark had her number and if he used it, she certainly wasn't going to let her machine answer. And he had a nice enough voice and was a little nervous, which meant he wasn't a serial womanizer. So Karen, unenthusiastic, changed dates on him twice but they eventually went out for a drink, a sexy idea if Karen had not forced it to a Sunday night.

In the dim light of the bar, Mark was not unattractive; he was plain, the way a girl is plain. He didn't seem to have any pronounced features but at the same time they weren't all so similar that he was handsome. His face was fat in every way, youthful: his nose was round, his cheeks were round but somehow his body was lean which gave him the look of someone you didn't really notice.

As they debated having another drink, he told a story about someone eating his lunch out of a refrigerator at work. It didn't matter who did it but he had an idea because he saw mustard on the sleeve of some receptionist. He told Karen that most guys say they're having lunch with clients but they always end up watching sports in a bar together and it's costly and a waste of time and he has an edge because he brings his own and usually he's the only guy awake in the afternoon. She laughed and he looked at her, his face kind of changing with surprise and he said, "People don't get me sometimes." For Karen, this was lovely.

Maybe they were meant to be together because she thought he was very funny. A lot of the stories had happened to him and he was frequently the butt of the joke. It was almost like he had the personality of someone very confident, someone who came off so strongly that they felt they had to constantly deprecate themselves. Still, his face said the opposite. They started dating and three or four weeks in, they had sex in his apartment because she might want to leave right after. But she didn't. His rooms were well appointed but not slick and his hands had held her waist so firmly that her hips were pleasantly sore, so she relaxed into his down pillows, soothing and familiar with the scent of lavender dryer sheets. And then they had sex again the same night and she felt that he desired her. And that was very attractive.

★

Mark's Father was a high school football coach and also an administrator and civics teacher so he had some status beyond sports in the upper middle class suburb of Newton, Massachusetts. With all the professional families and their well-bred but rebellious children, Mark slowly discovered who he really was: some version of the chauffeur's son. He had everything the others had but of lesser quality: an old-fashioned three-speed bicycle, no trading cards, unexciting and infrequent vacations and tennis shoes bought from the bin in the super-market.

His Father found him lacking in aggression and eventually gave up bullying him, finding him best suited for supporting the real warriors, like a girl. Mark did eventually show some athletic ability in cross-country running, which required psychological discipline but was solitary and dismissive of the teamwork his Father thought most valuable. By junior year Mark knew that he preferred to be quietly competitive and that he didn't get along with men because he hated the anonymous place they assigned him when they were in groups.

Women had been a mystery to Mark. His Mother was an eternal cheerleader and his older, smarter Sister had wrapped the family in the drama of an eating disorder in her early teens, her battle to delay adulthood finally won when she had a heart attack after returning from treatment at seventeen and died. In addition, he learned that he had none of his Father's charisma and his physical appearance, his face mostly, was no help to him in developing confidence with women.

He got attention for having a dead sister; still it was normal to him, and her long illness had made him so self-reliant that no girl could imagine his loneliness. His Sister's demise had most importantly made strangers of his parents, as they rarely spoke to him, instead retreating into the mundane: cleaning, painting and repairing the house so worn down by the failure of their years-long rescue mission. By his senior year in high school they had moved on to the yard where gardening allowed them to spend time on their knees in the dirt, no different than the wet vegetables they picked and let rot in baskets by the mudroom. Mark wondered if anything could ever relieve their silent, busy grief and resolved to be the achieving survivor for their benefit, but in equal measure he knew that massive financial success and a high, white collar job would allow him to be reborn into a world where none of this had ever happened.

Mark liked Karen because she had no idea how beautiful she was. She had raven hair and blue eyes and her body was fit yet still soft and curvy. When he asked his coworker who'd set them up how he could have left this detail out, the coworker revealed he'd never seen her. His wife knew her and said she was an 8, she'd actually said she was a 7 but he couldn't tell that to Mark, especially after Mark had openly declared her a 10. The coworker was pleased but curious and when he finally met Karen at the Christmas party he was confounded by the fact that she was indeed very beautiful, although not a 10, and she did have a great rack.

The night Mark and Karen finally undressed before each other, he stared at her as she got up to get a robe and go to the bathroom. It was a bright moonlit night and her nipples were almost purple in the blue air, her skin so milky, her thighs so full and ankles so narrow. He thought he would never get tired of having sex with her and he took that thought very seriously and knew they would marry.

*

You might think a man like Mark who was not rich by 40 would never be rich, but he worked in a field of finance where a big score was still possible. While Mark and Karen were engaged, there was a promotion available which included a bonus that would have catapulted him into wealth. Now that they were a couple and enjoying the social fruits of dining with other couples and the joy of guaranteed company on New Year's Eve and Valentine's, they held the unspoken status of being on the verge of success. The promotion hung in the balance throughout the entire planning of the wedding and both of them were thinking how much bigger a party they could throw but also worrying that it might not happen and they could be in debt and Mark might even have to find another job.

Karen was prepared to give up her years accrued in publishing because it was a repetitive, gossipy business and she rarely had contact with writers. Also, she wasn't exactly in publishing. It was the reason she came to New York, but the competition was impenetrable and so she migrated through temp work into the adjacent world of public relations, where in addition to the mild glamour of independent films and restaurant openings, she was brought tantalizingly close to a publishing house. Eventually, she told people she was in publishing because no one understood publicity, especially the freelance kind and someone had once misheard her and the reaction was noticeably more enthusiastic. Deeply behind the scenes, she booked travel and appearances for authors and editors and after once covering for her boss with a perfectly purchased apology of handmade chocolate and ash-striped cheese, she began to design themed gift baskets so specific and exquisite that many urged her to start her own business.

The praise she garnered in this unexpected sideline only highlighted her clear lack of enthusiasm and drive for the career she had fallen into. Unlike her boss, she was incapable of shaking her suburban manners or showing sudden charm to strangers with her sunglasses on her head and thus upon realizing that Mark might insist she change her profession to wife and mother, she was pleasantly excited. Karen knew that there were no housewives in Manhattan in the traditional sense and that she could be quite fulfilled by becoming a volunteer at the school, a nest builder, and a manager of servants.

When Mark was passed over two weeks before the wedding, Karen was crushed to the point that she debated if she could get out of it. As she sat in her kitchen in the middle of the night and wrote down the pros and cons on a piece of paper, she considered the horrible fact that maybe she was only marrying him for money. But she knew she was a better person than that. She knew that what she had come to know as love had become love when she was around him. She didn't just want to have a child before it was too late; she wanted to have a child with him. That was very important; in fact, it was the only thing on the list she'd made and she was glad for the whole exercise and wondered why she had never been brave enough to distill her ambition on paper before.

*

Mark did become rich by any standard other than his own. At work he was known for having the enviable skill of recognizing when an asset was distressed. With stocks, bonds, real estate and especially companies, he was able to substantiate through mathematical analysis the lack of value that made things vulnerable and frequently gave tips that made money or at least encouraged trades. Nevertheless, it was not his talent that enriched him in the end, but his luck at being part of a group that shared a gigantic commission from landing a university endowment. And damn it if missing that promotion hadn't almost ruined his wedding but he happened to be in the right place at the right time and they had a big year. And then they had another. And then they had another and he had plenty and there was no reason to worry anymore. He wasn't the richest guy in New York, but he could still do most of the things that they did except for appearing in magazines.

He of course wanted more, at least enough for a country place and one of those awards people got for being generous to causes, but he felt lucky that Karen didn't have social aspirations and took their wealth as a given as if she were born with it and had nothing to prove. He loved and even envied that about her and finally asked her about her natural inclination towards privacy and thus private satisfaction. One night, after a very expensive bottle of wine, while they lay spent in the after, Karen told Mark that other women had never used her as a measure because she easily re-ceded in groups, most comfortable as an approv-ing spectator. And yet she wondered to Mark, her voice soft, eyes welling, why this was not enough. She refused to gossip, having once been the sub-ject of a particularly vicious rumor that claimed she had arrived and stayed at a summer beach house share without being invited. This rumor then evolved into the insinuation that her nose or her breasts were fake, painting her permanently as desperate. Why they had singled her out was a mystery to her but most likely the group had decided she was perfect for shouldering their in-securities, her natural shyness and silence having been perceived as confidence. As she rested her head on his chest, clasping him with her naked-ness she revealed that like Mark, she had suffered from the cruelty of the mob, but she had come to understand that you could never see yourself the way others did, and it was okay to appear isolated as long as you remember that you are not the way you are seen.

Karen woke Mark on his 41st birthday with her head under the blankets and her mouth on him. After, when she came back from brushing her teeth, she curled up next to him and told him she was pregnant. Mark's enthusiasm was immediate despite his depleted state but his feelings deepened as Karen spoke in a strategic tone about their need for a larger apartment. She had planned for a week to deliver the news that way and was giddy with relief that he reacted with sufficient excitement.

Mark enjoyed all of it: he was giving beautiful Karen the life she wanted, he was creating a family, a legacy; and what he enjoyed most was her shift from carnal to practical in the course of a few minutes. It made him want her again although he wasn't sure if it was healthy in her condition. Karen laughed at him. She still thought he was funny and as they made love he noticed that her body had changed some to his liking. When she came he felt her drain of all anxiety as she disappeared into the warmth of expectation.

Karen's pregnancy was uneventful with the exception of their move to a ten-unit apartment building west of Park Avenue, an area known as one of the last real neighborhoods in Manhattan. The 3-bedroom had no balcony but was one floor below the penthouse and had a view over the rooftops of brownstones with almost nothing postwar in sight and there was a chain coffee shop or optician on every corner and a grocery store that felt like an old-time market and a few tall buildings, which still had shiny brass elevator doors.

The co-op board was rigid and testy, and stalled until Mark recused himself, allowing Karen's belly and glow to win them over. Their daughter was born at Lenox Hill Hospital at a reasonable hour and Mark was there and she was brought home to a stocked nursery and a few new friends Karen had made as she entered the world of birthing classes and stroller selection. They named her Heather. Mark liked that it reflected his Scottish heritage, but it was really a coincidence since Karen had picked it from a book, believing she had never met a Heather who was not beautiful.

Unlike her friends, Karen dismissed the baby nurse early, finding that breastfeeding, sleeplessness and tracking milestones were no burden to her. In fact she welcomed even the most extreme intrusions, viewing any contact, even at three in the morning, as an opportunity to touch and smell her baby. The pleasure of Heather overtook all others and she continued to refuse help as the baby grew, documenting every day with pictures and notes but never needing to show them to anyone because they were always together and Heather could be experienced firsthand. When Heather was four and finally entered the most caring and progressive nursery school, though not necessarily the most prestigious, it was Karen who spent the day crying. And as the days passed she would occupy those few hours while Heather was in school heartbroken in bed, then spring to life at pickup time when she could hold her daughter's hand again as they made cookies or watched videos or simply walked through the park.

*

About ten years before Mark and Karen's first date, Robert Klasky was born in Newark, New Jersey, to a single mother in the public hospital. Bobby, as he was called, was a miracle unnoticed by the medical staff, since they were unaware that his Mother had rarely consumed anything other than beer during her mostly unacknowledged pregnancy. He was born with his Mother's last name since his father could have been any number of people who had Bobby's mousy brown hair and blue eyes.

Bobby's Mother stayed in the hospital as long as permitted before returning to the small clapboard house in the town of Harrison, where she had spent most of her unhappy life. Harrison was originally filled with Polish immigrants and was now poor but still mostly white which was unusual for that part of New Jersey and would be quaint if not for the visual cues of poverty: the flimsy screen doors, mounds of garbage, strewn scrap metal and the black knit of telephone lines that cluttered the horizon.

Having Bobby did little to alter his Mother's belief that heroin was the best thing in her life. She had never intended to spend her adult years in Harrison with all the "lowlifes" as she called them. Despite her judgment, she took up with a series of bums, violent addicts and drunks who liked a meal and a roof and then a woman for kicks. Bobby had eaten cigarette butts and drunk beer before he was ten and even helped her boyfriends and some of their friends shoot up when they were too sick.

He was frequently awakened in the middle of the night and dragged into the living room, never knowing if he was going to be a punching bag or a parlor trick. His Mother survived on government assistance and stealing, especially in the good years when they were building the stadium and construction was everywhere, but she mostly worked in local beauty parlors sweeping up hair and sometimes as an unlicensed cosmetician, which was ideal since it allowed her to follow her soap operas, skim from the register and evaluate others' appearance with authority.

It was a relief to both Bobby and his Mother when he started school. He enjoyed it because it was structured and there was something to eat other than Taylor ham sandwiches, but soon he realized he was smarter than all of the students and most of the teachers. He discovered that he could get anything he wanted by simply telling the truth about his Mother or his poverty, particularly to the younger teachers whose eyes would fill with tears and buy him fast food and promise things would change. Nothing did, of course. The worst that would happen was his Mother would get a visit, but she was impossible to get in trouble because she had no shame and would frequently greet bureaucrats and do-gooders in her oversized T-shirt nightgown or a ratty kimono.

Bobby spent most of his time alone. It was hardest in the summer when the house was full of junkies and the TV had to be watched on mute. He would go down to the river which was littered with abandoned appliances and tires and feel lonely and sick because "he, too, felt thrown away," as a prison psychologist would one day tell him.

Nothing really held his interest except animals. They were like people to him, dumb and helpless, especially the roadkill he would pick up and hide in the garage for later inspection. Only by accident did Bobby finally discover his own power when he saw a bird trapped inside the window air conditioner and turned it on and watched in awe as the animal was battered by the fan until blood sprayed out the vent.

Bobby dropped out of high school and got a job at a lumberyard loading trucks and eventually pallets once he figured out the forklift. He continued to live at home after staking out his own room with a padlock and in his off-hours he would watch TV and drink vodka and absorb the meaningless talk and explosive laughter of his Mother's friends and lovers at her spontaneous nightly gatherings.

Sometimes a fight would break out and he would just leave and sit on the stoop or walk to the corner store for more beer. A neighbor girl, known as Chi-Chi, would frequently be on her stoop as well and he thought her very beautiful and could tell she was finding a way to talk to him. Once, on a particularly overcast Saturday afternoon, he crossed the street early so he could pass closer and said, "Nice sunny day, huh?" She smiled back and he was pleased that he had said one of those things people say.

TWO

MARK'S LIFE DIDN'T CHANGE much when Heather came along. At first there was little for him to do. Karen took care of everything and it made sense since he couldn't really feed the baby, preferred not to change diapers and was at work when all of the bathing and strolling was done. But eventually, he found that Karen and Heather lived as a closed unit and he was on the outside. His attempts to participate were thwarted by his ignorance and it was true that it was always easier for Karen to do things herself than to watch him struggle with dressing the toddler or loading the bag for a trip to the park.

He wasn't angry with Karen but with himself, taking his relegation to observer as an extension of flaws that were now equally apparent at the office. In the halls of finance, Mark had never been able to make himself essential. Although his work was adequate and he made more money than he had ever dreamed, he witnessed a string of undeserving men move past him with skills far more social than financial, and he gave up the thought that he would ever run the department or even fly on the company jet.

Heather was a beautiful baby. Her blonde hair would eventually darken but she had large blue eyes and she smiled as early as four weeks, often clapping her little fat hands with delight. Karen fitted her in French knits and found that although she was a girl, light blue suited her coloring and her temperament. Heather sought out others' eyes and won over even the most downbeat New Yorkers with her squeals and laughter.

She was so beautiful that when she would in-
evitably become the center of attention in a
park or a store, her newly won friends would
look at Karen, or Mark and Karen together,
and be unable to hide their surprise that this
child belonged to these people. Heather's parents were never insulted but shrugged with
humble pride, both of them having concluded
independently, though they never shared it with
each other, that their inner selves had been
expressed through their beautiful biological cre-
ation. Mark even mused to Karen that perhaps
they were "so good at making kids," maybe they
should have another.

★

As much as Karen loved her parents and considered her childhood in leafy suburban DC idyllic,
she remembered most of those years as lonely.
She always wanted a sibling and wondered,
because her Mother was obsessed with birth control, explaining it to her before she even understood what it was, if she was an accident. For
a while she had an imaginary brother ten years
older who would drive her places like the ice
cream store and ballet practice, but it only took

a sleepover or a ride home from school with another family for her to remember that she was lucky not to be fighting over everything in her house.

On the other hand, not fighting for anything might've been a liability. Karen was by nature easily controlled by other people and tentative about risks. She was never the first one to dive into the pool but preferred to watch a few people try it. Also, her Mother went back to school for library science when she was a toddler, and her Father, a patent attorney, was unable to take on all of the housekeeping and parenting duties that lapsed. He was in love with his work, frequently appropriating his clients' creativity as his own. He had fantasies of invention and would tinker but for the most part enjoyed having the neighbors see him walking in and out of the house with rolled-up blueprints under his arm, schematic drawings of electrical and chemical structures beyond his comprehension.

By the time her Mother got a job running the Clarksburg Bookmobile, Karen was out of day-care and spent so many afternoons tucked in a corner watching her Mother read to children that she held her books facing an imaginary audience until she was in second grade. When spending cuts threatened to shutter the bookmobile, the town passed a referendum of support and suddenly it wasn't just the kids who waved to her Mother and called her by her first name.

Karen hated sharing her and spending so much time with the babysitter, who was really the cleaning woman, and eventually took up any activity that kept her late at school. By junior high, she had been ignored into full self-reliance and established a routine of locking herself in her room after school with a portable TV where she could escape to the saturated worlds of romance while having access to her body.

Karen told Mark she didn't want another child. It wouldn't be fair to Heather. In fact, Karen knew the minute Heather was born that she would give her uninterrupted attention and care for as long as possible. She never worried that she was justifying her lack of interest in a career or her reliance on Mark's success, because Heather was not an average child. Perhaps if Karen had shown the spark and magic that Heather did, her Mother would've never gone back to school.

★

As Heather grew into a little girl, her beauty became more pronounced but somehow secondary to her charm and intelligence and, most notably, a complex empathy that could be profound. "Why are you crying?" she said at five years old from her stroller to a Woman on the subway who was not crying and who corrected her politely. Heather continued, "You shouldn't be sad even if your bags are heavy. I can carry one." The Woman then laughed nervously and sat down next to Karen as she said she could handle her things, but thank you. Karen lightly scolded her child to mind her own business and handed her a sippy cup.

The Woman was looking up, pretending to read the ads, as Heather, still staring, removed the cup from her lips and said, "Everybody riding on the train acts like they're alone, but they're not." At that point the Woman burst into tears. Karen didn't know what to do and her search for a tissue became simply rubbing the woman's shoulder as she sobbed and awkwardly smiled, embarrassed. Heather watched both of them and by 77th Street when they had to get off, she said byebye and the Woman, now composed, looked at Karen and said that she must be the best mother in the world. Karen deferred the credit to her child and although it looked like modesty, she knew that Heather did things like this all the time and that she was somehow here on earth to make people feel better.

For Karen there was plenty to do every day even after Heather began a full day of school. There was exercise and shopping, not a lot of housework that wasn't done by someone else, activities and enrichments to discover and investigate, nutritious meals and thoughtful entertainment to be planned, and of course, documenting the daily wonder of Heather could never be ignored. Karen made scrapbooks, collages on the computer and with some effort, little movies that she could share on the Internet. She worried at first that she was bragging in some way, but when she saw that everyone responded to her daughter the way she did, she knew that she was actually brightening people's day and that maybe they, like her, were learning so much about themselves as they watched Heather grow.

In the communities she visited online, she found so many like-minded women and got such encouragement that any worry was quickly abated either by a veteran mom or an actual expert. This meant that Karen spent less time around other people in general, but she was always open to interacting, and from the beginning, whether they were strolling in the park or swimming at the club or eventually playing tennis, Heather made Karen game for sitting down and having a snack with anyone.

*

The Breakstone family, small as it was, used more than its share of resources and Mark was proud that he was able to provide them with a beautiful apartment. He particularly liked Karen's taste for satin velvet, which was used sparingly but seemed directly aimed at him. They had a velvet headboard on their bed and a suite in the living room featuring an armchair of the same that he favored on his increasingly sleepless nights, preferring it to his private paneled study where the furniture was cold leather. The living room chair was red but appeared brown in the dark and he would pour a few fingers of scotch in the best glass and be able to either doze off or at least not be nervous about seeing the sunrise or how the long night would make his workday unbearable.

One late night while Mark was preparing for his chair he realized that he could look in on Heather, now seven, while she slept. He was never alone with his daughter and felt his wife's resentment when he would sit down at the dinner table and say, "How are my girls today?" He had arrived at the phrase because when he would talk to Heather directly, Karen would always answer for her or insinuate herself into the conversation. Even when Heather was sick, his "How are you feeling, piglet?" was answered by Karen. "She's better, thank God" or "She had a crappy day." So that night, when he found himself standing in her room staring at her, he felt guilty and strange when she opened her eyes and smiled at him. He couldn't explain why he was there so he just sat on the bed and stroked her hair. He finally said, "Why are you up?" and she said, "Because I can't sleep. I must be like you." He brushed her fore-head and gave her a kiss on the cheek and said, "Where do you want to go on vacation? We can go anywhere." And Heather said, "Wherever you are, Daddy."

That year, instead of going to St. Bart's, Karen and Mark, at Heather's request, agreed to go to Orlando as long as they could stay at the luxury hotel that was not dominated by the theme park. They had a suite with a living room for their daughter's rollaway and despite Heather con-stantly picking up annoying friends, the family enjoyed the mix of crowds followed by intimate dinners. One night Heather insisted on hanging out in the game room and Mark and Karen found themselves alone. In their anxiety they got drunk and made love but were up and worrying again by ten o'clock when Heather returned as promised. They had not made love in a long time, what with Karen swamped with Heather's dance, tennis and piano lessons and Mark's increasing insom-nia which had taken him from their bed almost every night.

———

The next morning was rainy, so while Karen had a massage, father and daughter took a crafts class and Mark and the other guests basked in the sunshine Heather created with her laugh and willingness to help the smaller children. Before they left they quickly made a beaded necklace for Karen so she would not feel left out. Mark and Karen got drunk and did it again that night while Heather slept in the next room and it was somehow less but followed by a whispered conversation about how long they'd been together and what a miracle Heather was. The last day the three of them sat far from the breakfast buffet, overlooking the man-made lagoon, so conspicuously happy that a passing woman insisted she take a picture for them.

*

While the Breakstone family was on vacation, Bobby was laid off from the lumberyard. He was told he would get his job back and they had let everyone go for a few weeks only to rehire them to avoid some labor laws and he was happy to spend some of the money he'd been earning or maybe go somewhere. But his Mother had broken up with her latest and Bobby agreed to give her a loan so she could feed her habit, knowing full well he would never see the money again. It didn't matter because where would he go anyway and wandering around Harrison and Newark would be fine in the spring before it got sticky. He also had become increasingly interested in Chi-Chi across the street. Her brother was a mechanic and told him that her real name was Chiquita and that she was older than he thought. They were from Mexico and there was other stuff that Bobby ignored because all he wanted to know was that she had noticed him and that she was alone most of the time when he walked by.

One day he went out for beer and his heart raced when Chi-Chi stepped onto the porch in a light blue dress. That was his favorite color and it suited her brown skin and there was lace around the neck almost like a nightgown. As he approached her side of the street he slowed and nodded to her. She smiled back and he stopped. He had never stopped before, but she had never really smiled before and somehow she must have known that was his favorite color. He walked up the steps offering her a beer as he did, but she simply turned her back and opened the screen door for him and went inside. He followed quickly, but then she stopped near the stairs and asked him to leave. Bobby didn't know what kind of game she was playing so he put down the beer and told her how pretty she was and how happy he was to see her every day. She smiled again, but he could see her face was twitching a little and it was clear she was scared and that really pissed him off, especially as she tried to move past him to the front door. He held her and told her to stop everything she was doing. She could be scared if she wanted but he didn't care because he knew what she wanted. He grabbed her hair and shoulders but she slipped away and picked up an ashtray from the seat of a chair and hit him in the temple. His vision was white for a moment as he stared at her. He screamed at her as he took her arm and twisted it, "Don't you know who I am?" She started to cry and struggle and finally he just punched her in the stomach while he still held her arm and he felt her body give way. She flew back to the wall and he punched her again, this time on the side of her head. And as she dropped to the ground unconscious, he caught his breath and looked around so panicked that only later did he remember he had been rubbing himself through his pants to calm down. He picked up the beer and ran home, locking himself in his room and drinking half a bottle of vodka until he could sleep.

He told his Mother to tell people he wasn't there if someone was looking for him. He wasn't sure if Chiquita's brother would show up or if she was dead. But why did she do that? Why were the pretty ones always so dumb? It kept rolling over in his head, washed out only by his Mother's screams as she tried to block the police from his bedroom door. His Mother was worried about her stash so she put up a valiant defense but Bobby just opened his door and calmly went along, stunned by the whole afternoon's events. What was hardest to believe was that Chi-Chi would press charges when they were selling OxyContin out of her house and she had a brother who weighed 220 pounds and was perfectly capable of dealing with Bobby on his own.

It was the first time Bobby was in jail and he kept to himself and even got some antibiotics for where the ashtray cut his head, which was already infected. Chiquita was alive and the Public Defender, who was impressed by him he could tell, laughed at the idea of the State getting him for attempted murder. Things went according to plan and Bobby watched the court playing around him as if it were a TV show. He eventually pled out to assault and mustered some emotion that sounded like regret and before Bobby was remanded, the Public Defender told him that he would do three not five years and that it was a chance to change. It wasn't until Bobby went to prison in Trenton that he learned how lucky he was that Chiquita's concussion kept her from remembering he was there to rape her. This all could have been so much worse.

★

Mark had only been with a few women in his life and none of them, other than Karen, had he chosen or pursued. After suffering through numerous rejections in high school, including one girl who rebuffed his advances by revealing that the origin of his class-given nickname, "Moonstone," was not a play on Breakstone but referred to the shape of his face, Mark withdrew socially, discovered cross-country running and satisfied himself to yearbook pictures and catalogues since pornography embarrassed him.

When he lost his virginity in college it was a joy to wake up next to real flesh and she was kind about his performance and they fell into the habit even though he wasn't attracted to her at all. She wasn't ugly but a little heavy and the first of all the women he slept with before Karen, who were loud, brash and loose and seduced him with an air of charity. For his part he was expected to quietly support their unrealistic dreams of clothing design or magazine writing while taking their side in disputes, especially against all other women who were clearly envious.

Mark remained filled with longing and grew to hate intercourse after the first time with any of them so he entered the workplace celibate, hoping that either his salary or what age did to his face would attract another kind of woman. He only agreed to be set up as a bonding experience with the leering former jocks in his office. He would, as demanded, announce his successes with these increasingly desperate women but then back away, having never revealed himself to anyone and finding the ultimate prize of sex alienating when won with false intimacy. He was well aware of how much Karen had changed his life so many years ago. In fact, he reminded himself of this often ever since the new Trainee, an Asian girl of 26, had started asking for his coffee order.

There were so few women in Mark's office that any female presence became the object of fantasy, plus the Trainee was an MBA and one of those new kind of girls who mistakenly thought that talking crudely and explicitly was a feminist imperative. Her mouth did not give her any power but instead made her a kind of dog toy for the managers, who sent her for coffee while they critiqued her outfits with graphic instant messages. Mark of course did not participate but he was equally intrigued, aroused at times to the point of imagining the Trainee when he and Karen would eventually make love.

The path to Mark and Karen's bedroom had become increasingly filled with obstacles despite their vow to spend more time in each other's arms after Orlando. They had started with a designated date night although both eventually had conflicts, Mark with work and Karen with Heather, now 12 years old, needing her attention with her academic and social life at their tony all-girls prep school.

Despite the fact that Heather continued to be popular and an excellent student, Mark agreed with Karen that she should have supplementary tutors in all subjects in addition to her other assorted lessons. This schedule was exhausting for Karen but allowed her to monitor Heather's friendships which required real attention since Heather was not critical of people and was frequently taken advantage of by clingy and maladjusted girls who used her to advance socially or as a sounding board for their self-centered dramas. So as date night faded away in a series of mutual cancellations, Karen was apologetic and Mark pretended to be spurned but understanding, although he was relieved, burdened by the fact that when he didn't think about the Trainee, he was unable to perform.

———

When the Trainee closed the door to Mark's office one day, she was quickly in tears, wondering what she was doing wrong and why no one took her seriously. He felt a wave of heat in his head that became sweat and he stammered until she composed herself and, wiping her eyes, whispered that he was the only good thing about the stupid place and left. Mark knew his response to her statements had been honorable but he also knew what had really transpired and that he might capitalize on her feelings sometime in the near future with little fear of rejection.

Mark went home early and sat in the kitchen until Heather and Karen finally came home. They had grabbed dinner after playing an impromptu game of tennis following Heather's lesson and he could not control the volume of his voice as he told Karen that he had eaten nothing and would no longer tolerate being the last thing on her mind and that this was a family and he was part of it and why the hell couldn't he eat dinner or play tennis with Heather?

———

Heather watched teary-eyed from the living room even though she had been ordered to leave and Karen, having never thought about any of this, was stricken with remorse and promised things would change. She offered the solution that Saturday morning would be father-daughter time and that she had been thoughtless. That night Mark had a dream that the Trainee and Heather were eating lunch with him in his speeding car and that Heather had suddenly opened the door and jumped out.

The next morning Mark realized that age had not improved his looks at all. His hair was there but he had gained weight and when he had finally figured out Karen's body-fat calculating scale, he saw that he was 22 pounds heavier than he was in high school and most of it was in his cheeks and jowls. He decided to start running again, the benefits being that his thoughts about the Trainee disappeared and with the exception of the first few days of spring, when Central Park was littered with pale half-dressed girls, he had no sexual feelings at all and would finish each day exhausted and calm.

———

His greatest satisfaction became his one weekend day alone with Heather. Their trips to the movies or the museum or shopping were always memorable because funny things happened to Mark, like getting his foot stepped on by a horse near the Plaza Hotel, and Heather, with her natural smile and tomboy energy, always managed to create a stir with strangers and the two of them rarely left anyplace without someone giving her something for free.

★

Within days of arriving at the New Jersey State Prison, Bobby was administered mandatory psychological tests and recruited by the white supremacist gang upon the discovery of his Polish surname. He was then given a close haircut and a thorough beating in a room just off the showers as his initiation. He didn't understand at first that he was merely to receive the punches, kicks and head butts of the assembled six skinheads and he fought back, his strength surging in a flurried frenzy of strikes that stunned them. He finally lost consciousness as one sat on his chest, but the rain of blows and the entire engagement had made him feel his body as if for the first time, and the sight of his involuntary erection as he passed out earned him some wary distance and the nickname "Hard On" for the rest of his stay.

Bobby had no patience for the gang, especially since their major topic of conversation was not racial supremacy but the law. None of them thought they belonged there, at least for the thing that had actually gotten them incarcerated, and they used words like "incarcerated" and were more predictable even than the people on the outside. He did overhear some information that made him sure that if he had killed Chi-Chi, he wouldn't have done any time at all, since she was the only witness and he'd never actually left sperm behind, and he had no record except truancy and loitering and a shoplifting thing when he was a minor. He knew now that he should have killed her and then stolen a few things to make it look like robbery and make sure to get rid of the stuff in the garbage, not fence it, no matter how valuable it was. All their other conversation was unchanging complaints, pathetic to Bobby, who liked the food and his job in the laundry where he could sometimes roll around in the warm linens.

Bobby didn't exactly like prison but it was organized and he learned a lot. Due to a lapse in bureaucratic momentum and the inaccurate assumption that he would insist on a white doctor due to his gang affiliation, it took months to process his tests and realize he should be examined by a psychiatrist. It was in a room with blue carpet, which excited Bobby after all the linoleum and cinder block. He planned to approach it as he had with lady social workers, by telling his true story and trying to make them cry. But the Doctor was handsome like a TV star and not too old and matter-of-fact and Bobby could tell he was afraid.

He asked Bobby about his life, how he felt about himself and what made him happy and Bobby told the saddest version he could, looking down at the end of sentences and mentioning his walks by the filthy Passaic River. Most of the Doctor's questions were about how Bobby felt about other people. Bobby wanted to say the truth, that the outside world reminded him of a zoo where the animals are standing in their own shit and he just watches them with pity and curiosity as they squawk at each other, but instead he said he didn't think about it.

The Doctor then got blunt and tough and sort of suggested some things that Bobby, seeking more information, pretended not to understand. The Doctor said that Bobby was smart and knew he was smart and was a good-looking kid who liked to lie because it was easier. The Doctor was probably trying to make Bobby violent, especially when he stood up and said the game was over and Bobby should stop thinking that he was above any social dynamic and that Bobby understood how people behaved but it didn't factor into his life because he didn't think he had to follow the same set of rules. The Doctor finally sat down for emphasis and said, "If you can't change, control yourself. You can do anything."

Bobby left the session happy and filled with the anticipation of something, his idea of himself finally joining with what he actually was. Whether it was someone else's dessert, a nice car he saw in a magazine or the girl in the bikini next to it, he was aroused constantly now just thinking about the things he could have. What the Doctor said was all true to Bobby; he was so damn smart that people bored him and he was a bright light among them with all the power in heaven, and he could rape them and kill them anytime he wanted because that's why they were on earth.

During his Mother's only visit, after he had convinced her that he had no money, he asked her if she always knew what he was. He tried to explain as clearly as possible, that he was smart and powerful, etc., but he cut his explanation short, seeing she was confused, and they sat there a moment in the visiting room. She stared at him before saying, "Who the hell do you think you are?" Bobby greeted her question the way he had her thousand slaps to his face, smiling in answer since there was no point.

THREE

AT 55 YEARS OLD, Mark's maximum disinterest in his wife coincided with his daughter entering puberty. Karen later pointed out all of Heather's physical changes, but Mark didn't really notice much other than her gaining in height on her mother. What he did notice was that there was a discord between Karen and Heather, heated at first and then icy cold, and Mark felt a tension so strong that it eclipsed his discomfort with his wife. Mark could see that Karen felt useless as their daughter became more private and her secrecy more aggressive, but for Mark, who spent less time with her in general, it was happily not that different.

———

Father-daughter weekend time was canceled more than once but if Mark didn't react Heather would assure him that it would continue or even make up for it with a diner breakfast during the week. And Heather was not as hostile towards him even though she didn't share as much once he refused to join in conversations critical of Karen. Mark felt participating in such a discussion was worse than cheating and he knew instinctively that his daughter was best served by having him be her father and not her chum or confidant. So they would talk about the movies they'd seen or how much the city had changed or most importantly what vacation they'd take next because Mark wanted to lock Heather into any future plans with some kind of emotional investment since he couldn't imagine a trip without her.

One morning Mark discovered that Heather was no longer a child when she asked for a cup of coffee. Karen hated coffee and assumed her daughter merely wanted to appear mature, but Mark worried it was something else. He remembered that his Sister had started her terminal dieting with coffee, eventually graduating to mugs of hot water, which made her feel full and helped her equation of thinness, which was calories consumed measured against time so that every moment she wasn't eating she was gaining by losing more of her awful self.

He finally agreed to the coffee if there was a muffin or something as well and he totally gave up on the comparison when he watched his daughter eat, knowing that she greeted her plate with an enthusiasm that no one with an eating disorder could fake. She did remind him of his Sister in other ways, especially her lanky walk, but she never regarded her body with disgust and Mark knew that unlike his Sister, who had starved to avoid breasts and menstruation and men, Heather would be a normal teenage girl, and that was no comfort either.

Soon there would be boyfriends. He'd seen them on the way to school, some with loosened neckties, the rest in hooded sweatshirts, stinking of spicy deodorant with condoms in their wallets and he knew they would try to climb on Heather and then scramble when they heard him come in and call him "sir." Mark knew that he wanted to be a grandfather and of course see her happily married, but she would eventually be out of his life one way or another and he became so preoccupied with the near future that he feared he was wasting their special weekend days together by taking too many pictures and reminiscing about moments even as they were happening.

Heather learned to make great coffee, fine-tuning the grinder and rinsing the carafe beforehand with extra hot water, and Karen would get up early and buy baked things for them but sensed she was not welcome and started going to the gym instead. Mark and Heather's sleepy sipping and nibbling was routine and wordless but they were at peace together and this seemed to bring out an energetic pettiness in Karen.

For Christmas, Karen bought Mark a 1,200-dollar handmade Italian espresso machine that came with video instructions because it never worked the same way twice. Mark was excited and touched before Karen warned that it was too dangerous for

Heather to use and too complicated for Mark and since she was the only one who had seen the demonstration, she could and would make their coffee from now on. To which Heather said, "Jesus, that's pathetic." And for the first time Mark silently agreed.

★

After three and a half years Bobby found himself outside the prison walls but forced to return home. New Jersey had a release policy that provided no "gate money" or new clothes or job training or travel, instead offering enrollment for welfare and food stamps, a discount on a bus or train ticket and an opportunity to register to vote. Bobby's Mother picked him up in a Jeep Cherokee belonging to her new Boyfriend, a handsome drunk ex-greaser. Bobby arrived home to find no TV or computer, the kitchen appliances gone, the carpet pulled up and one of the bathrooms completely devoid of fixtures. They were methodically dismantling the house, trading each piece for pills which they parlayed into heroin.

———

His Mother and her Boyfriend spent most of their time in the dark because all of the lamps were in the bedroom where they were trying to grow marijuana. Bobby's old room was just as he left it except now it was their bedroom and they let him have it back for a bit rent-free until his assistance came in. The blood-flecked sheets and red Solo cups turned his stomach as he curled up to sleep that first night, too exhausted to plan beyond finishing the bottle of vodka they'd left on the phone books that acted as a nightstand. He hadn't had a real drink for years and as the warmth spread through his chest into his face he was overcome with the peace of not being in prison and listened with tears in his eyes to the trees rustling right outside his window in the late winter wind.

Bobby's Parole Officer gave long encouraging speeches about seizing opportunity and was always good for 50 dollars and a Big Mac. The Officer was young, black, and truly helpful when he realized that Bobby was a skinhead only in appearance. He had even intervened at the lumber supply to get Bobby his old job back, verifying that the crime was aggravated assault and not theft and that Bobby's release was on positive terms.

One day Bobby had to break up a fight between his Mother and her Boyfriend and showed up with a black eye and eventually revealed to the Officer that, although sharing heroin had begun their romance, their habits had grown and forced them to ruthlessly compete over every score. The Officer said Bobby was a survivor and urged him to get away from the house as soon as possible.

Bobby had told him too much but this man really cared about him and after the police became involved weeks later, another nightly party ending badly, the Officer was adamant about Bobby saving up and moving on. How could he be expected to "rise like a phoenix out of the ashes," the Officer asked, if he was "living in such a depraved environment?" Bobby knew this was true and limited his expenses to three pairs of coveralls, good boots, his third of the rent and a couple of handles of vodka a week.

———

The lumber supply store hadn't changed and his contact with the women customers was limited to long stares as they searched the aisles for light-bulbs or caulk. From his perch on the forklift he watched them wandering, clearly searching for men and not finding anything they deserved, like rope, or gloves, or him. He behaved himself, never even following one beyond the parking lot and was satisfied with roaming the old neighbor-hood, ducking behind cars or lying by the river to take them cruelly in his mind.

In Harrison, teachers and artists had moved in so now Bobby only had to worry about being robbed by the junkies at home and kept 2,300 dollars hidden in the lining of his coat. He wore the jacket all the time and even locked it in the bathroom with him when he showered. Sometimes he got un-dressed and ran the water as he counted the bills and imagined moving somewhere there were girls, not just gay boys and old Polacks, and in that new place maybe he would buy a car and rent a room with a little refrigerator where he could keep his drinks cold as he watched TV.

———

In mid-July a storm came with extreme heat and wilting humidity and his need to wear his coat aroused such suspicion that his Mother's Boyfriend crept into his room at night and punched Bobby in the head until his slumber became unconsciousness. He woke a day later drenched in sweat and dizzy, having missed work, and wandered into the kitchen to find his Mother spaced out with a black eye and two days' worth of dope clutched in her hand which was all that was left of her Boyfriend. She was so disoriented that despite his headache, Bobby was able to shoot it all into her and wait for her to convulse and pass out before putting her in a full bath and setting the house on fire by dragging the lit barbecue into the living room.

From an emergency room bed, Bobby told the Police how he had awakened in the smoke-filled house after being badly beaten and robbed by his Mother's Boyfriend. Having investigated both parties on numerous occasions, the Police concluded that this was an inevitable outcome. Bobby decided not to press charges and this helped his

Parole Officer relocate him for his safety, and now wiser, Bobby knew not to tell him how he longed for a chance to kill his Mother's Boyfriend or to brag to him about the way he had actually risen from a fire.

★

When she saw that Heather, now 13, was changing, first growing taller and leaner and then her breasts beginning to develop, Karen jumped in with delighted concern and took her bra shopping, reliving her own adolescence and sharing the wisdom that these changes were indeed for the better. Behind the transparent shower curtain that served as the dressing room of Madame Olga's brassiere boutique, they laughed like girlfriends, the foreign woman cupping and tucking Heather for a custom and indisputable fit. Karen even bought Heather a gift certificate that would allow her to buy more bras as she grew without dragging old Mom along.

Heather was given a cell phone and allowed to stay out later and was even driven to Philadelphia to see a loud, drug-filled rock concert. Still, Karen wondered if her magnanimous anticipation of Heather's rebellion actually triggered it because it came in a tidal wave just weeks later. Chores and phone calls were ignored, curfew was broken, makeup was stolen, and Heather's hygiene first lapsed and then became extreme with two showers a day.

During the next year Heather found catastrophic uses for her newly acquired power like quitting all her lessons and failing to hear her Mother's voice so often that Karen took her to an audiologist. One night after being admonished for eating dinner with headphones around her neck, Heather calmly walked to her room and slammed the door and a silence set in. Suddenly all talk was small talk, and nothing, not the weather, not the election, not even the saltiness of the soup could be dealt with in more than one word.

This silence created such an anxiety in Karen that even after a month of looking at her daughter's phone while she slept, her dread could not be abated. The arrival of Heather's period was discovered sometime later when Karen found a box

of tampons under the guest room sink and realized that the tearful speech she had prepared
about the future wonders of motherhood and
married love had long expired, leaving her with
nothing more to offer than practical advice like
not to flush things down the toilet.

Since Heather's very first day of school, Karen
would hang out at drop-off with the other moms,
all in their exercise clothes debating which coffee
place to go to or whether to go at all, and the
bragging was constant. Even though Karen had
the most to brag about, she still left these inter-
changes feeling inadequate and inarticulate and
unarmed. She also found that if they did go to
coffee or lunch, it would always be in a group and
she never picked the restaurant and her attempts
at leading the conversation through topic or emotion were always ignored. And although she knew
that by not being there she would become the
topic, and that people who bragged were expressing their own insecurities which she was bringing
out in them, none of this could dispel the awful
feeling that she had about being the third, fourth,
or probably fifth wheel. It seemed best that she
skip the whole thing and so she never ran for Par-

ents' Association or volunteered anything more than paper plates. Her services would clearly be unwanted and unneeded and, she anticipated, ultimately unrewarded.

Karen's suspicions were confirmed when right before Heather's elementary school graduation, one of the moms invited her along for a stationary bicycle workout. As they approached the studio on 83rd Street and Third Avenue, she casually suggested that Mark and Karen underwrite the entire cost of the grad night skating party and dinner dance. She reasoned to Karen with a smile that she knew they were a busy family and that they should participate in the school in some way. After all, they didn't want to embarrass Heather, did they? Karen made it halfway through the workout before her pulse exceeded the bicycle's heart monitor and she left in what she eventually discovered was a full-blown panic attack.

This new distance from Heather was unbearable alone, and even Karen's own Mother had just laughed at it all and said Heather would be fine. So after a brief course of psychotherapy that predictably turned into an irritating discussion of her own childhood, Karen became angry and moody herself. She began to provoke her daughter with arbitrary rules and excessive punishment and withholding money and even had mock conversations where she played both parts and imitated her daughter's monotone. Finally, one night, after Heather had been forced to cancel a sleepover because it was snowing, she appeared in the doorway of Karen's bedroom and said, "I know you don't want me to have friends because you don't have any and you're afraid I'll abandon you," and then walked away. Heather's empathy had matured with the rest of her and was now incisive to the point of pain.

Karen stopped sleeping and would lie awake alone since Mark had taken permanently to the couch. She was heartsick with memories of her little girl in their bed, sweating through a fever or sobbing in the aftermath of a bad dream or whispering to herself as her dolls navigated the terrain of the comforter. Once in Central Park, as they picked up their iced coffees at the restaurant near the sailboats, Karen dropped her purse and the contents spilled across the cement. A young French tourist couple began to help them gather the things and at that moment Heather said, "Thank you so much. My friend is a little clumsy." Karen became so emotional that Heather blanched, fearing that she'd hurt her mother irreparably. God, Heather was so beautiful and Karen was there for her but still let her be independent and no one laughed more and thank God Heather was modest because too much attention did not make nice people. Only now did Karen realize she had reacted that way because all she had ever wanted was for Heather to be her friend.

As much as Karen hated the loss of what had been, what she really hated was that Mark was reaping the rewards of all her hard work, exaggerating his own conflicts with their daughter when for the most part they enjoyed each other's company and their shared interests of coffee and shopping and letting her do whatever she wanted.

*

The real trouble at the Breakstones' started when a hedge fund manager with a wife and two sons bought the penthouse. They planned to gut the unit and offered their new neighbors a 6-month reduction in fees if they could run a chute from their future kitchen down to a dumpster during demolition. The usually obstructionist building board offered a compromise to their newest, most generous occupant and the hedge fund manager agreed to take advantage of this moment of inconvenience to personally refurbish the entire building's exterior as well. There was both jealousy and suspicion in the elevators, but within weeks, scaffolding cloaked the whole edifice and all but a few families chose to relocate.

Mark knew that Karen would be most affected by daytime construction but his suggestion of a furnished sublet in the Carlyle House revealed that Karen was clearly not interested in such a drastic though temporary change and was overwhelmed by even having to redirect the mail. So they stayed in the building with the option of leaving if the interruptions of water and power or the constant noise became too much of a hardship. Heather did not have a vote but they deluded themselves that they would sacrifice their comfort so that she could have the consistency of life essential to teenage well-being.

———

The beauty of autumn in New York was not lost on Mark although soon it became evident that this fall would be as bleak as the longest February. The day after Labor Day he received a discouraging memo regarding year-end bonuses, and then a week later the construction battle was fought and lost. The worst of it was that Heather had begun ninth grade by enthusiastically joining the debate team, and her afternoons and weekends were occupied by practices and tournaments, sometimes out of town.

She was good at it and was becoming political and argumentative even though her natural charm made everything she said seem reasonable. She was still good-natured and talkative with him but completely obsessed and he hated that her coffee was taken to go in the expensive thermos Karen bought her and that she traveled to Buffalo and Chicago and Dallas on commuter planes. Most of all he hated that there were hotel overnights with co-ed carousing, every team trip marked by some incident, never involving Heather, but older girls, alcohol and room-hopping.

———

Heather assured him that she was still irritated by boys and preferred her girls' school where no one had to hide that they were smart or ambitious to get a boyfriend and Mark realized that all of Heather's thoughts were deeply reasoned and presented as positions to be defended. He started reading the newspaper to keep up with her since his opinions were often dated and based on statistics long since disproved. He loved their new intellectual engagements, no matter how hotly argued, because he was often truly humbled by her logic and proud that a girl raised in that world, at those schools, could have such deep economic empathy.

The only subject off-limits was the building, because Heather was excited by the changes but Mark was angry at the disaster of noise and dust, believing it to be his fault. He had brought the construction on all of them by never making enough money to buy the penthouse himself or, more importantly, failing to earn his way to 5th Avenue where there were no such problems and you could look out on Central Park and remember only the pleasures of childhood.

———

Two weeks into construction Karen began planning for Heather's fourteenth birthday, which included many unnecessary trips to various bakeries and restaurants for firsthand inspection. Upon making reservations at two different spots, she texted her daughter to ask if she preferred French or Italian for her birthday dinner. A few minutes passed and Karen realized that she wasn't going to get an answer for a long time and she began walking down Lexington Avenue at a brisk pace composing other texts in her head about how she had made a reservation for four so that a friend could join and how they couldn't eat at the house because of the dust and how she didn't want to celebrate anything in there and what else could she say, it was Heather's goddamn birthday, was Heather coming to dinner or not?

When Karen burst into the apartment, the extreme heat sent from the basement had not been adjusted for the unseasonably warm weather, and she quickly ran to the kitchen, where she had closed the window because of the noise, and opened it wide, vowing never to close it again.

71

The kitchen was still bright, too close to the next building for scaffolding, and as Karen caught her breath, she lingered in the low window, her hands on the narrow sill, looking down at the ten-story fall, contemplating the dramatic possibilities for permanent change.

She recognized the panic and after taking two antihistamines with a glass of white wine she sat at the kitchen table and made the second list of her life, one column labeled "Reasons for Being," the other "Reasons for Not." Could Heather still be at the top of the positives? Somehow clarity slipped in and Karen began to carefully consider other paths to purpose, including returning to work in publicity or getting plastic surgery to lift her breasts and her eyes. She knew that these were good enough plans to get her through Heather's adolescence and that an attitude of independence, no matter how false, would serve her well when her daughter had matured and come back to her. She also knew as she studied the paper that Mark was absent as a reason for anything.

★

Upon leaving Harrison, Bobby had close to 1,200 dollars, some from the government death benefit and some from a collection made at the lumberyard as a condolence for his poor Mother. With the aid of his Parole Officer, Bobby looked for new work in a different place and ended up in a long-term motel in North Bergen near the area called Routes 1 and 9. It was a good place for picking up work since it was a federal highway with no tolls and emptied out near the Holland Tunnel, turning the whole strip into a run-down garage and toolshed for New York City. He took the advice of the clerk who rejected his application at the home store and stood in the parking lot with the men and boys who waited for any one of a series of trucks to pick them up for 50-dollar-a-day work. Being young and strong was not enough to guarantee being selected so he began to imitate the Mexicans who smiled gratefully even though they weren't happy and never shared their morning beers and spoke Spanish in front of him like he wasn't there.

Lining up every day including weekends meant that Bobby started to work regularly and save

money and also that he could perhaps be a permanent part of a Manhattan crew. He had not spent
much time there outside of class trips and the cir-
cus and was excited by the commute from the
moment the city came into view in the distance
to when they made the turn uptown out of the
tunnel and he suddenly saw the huge buildings
up close. The city was so organized, so perfectly
blocked in rows, every steel box filled with a glass
box; even the cars were mostly black and square
and the same. Bobby's favorite part was after they
passed the leafy park with the cops on horseback
and they could pick up enough speed so he could
feel the rhythm between streets as they crossed
avenues with quick blasts of sky.

On the sidewalks though, Bobby felt nervous and
watched so many people pass without eye contact
that it recalled his first weeks in prison. Adding to
his discomfort were the smells, not the diesel or
garbage but the constant waft of human odor, as
seemingly all strangers' skin and breath reeked of
onions and vomit. The constant foot traffic and
general chaos of the new job site made it impossible for Bobby to avoid interactions with these
aromas as old ladies breathed dumb questions in

his face while they held plastic bags full of warm
dog shit. He was often so sick from the stench of
mothballs and human rot that he would hide in
the gutted top-floor apartment, usually above the
deck, so he could be alone with the view and the
tarpaper fumes.

It was from his rooftop spot in the late afternoon
that Bobby first caught the faint traces of a scent
that made him drop his coffee and inhale. His
nose and lungs filled with a mix of cigarettes, soap
and blood that exploded from a tall skinny girl
talking on her phone, smoke curling around her
shoulder-length light brown hair as if she were on
fire. For someone else it would have seemed that
time had stopped, but Bobby had no concept of
time so things were either interesting or boring
and when it came to people, either threatening or
arousing.

He watched her knowing she thought she was
alone on the roof as she unrolled the waist of her
plaid skirt to cover more of her soft thighs and
chomped on mints to prepare for her return to
the building. Bobby looked at the girl and felt a

yearning so powerful he thought he might faint or ejaculate.

The truck left right at five o'clock that night which meant he wouldn't see the girl again that day, but it hadn't been hard to figure out who she was since there were only two or three families still living in the building and the mail was stacked on a table in the demolished lobby. She was named Karen or Heather Breakstone, lived on the tenth floor, and loved catalogues and magazines with perfume in them.

Bobby spent the ride back emotional, cursing himself for not taking a picture on his phone while trying to rebuild her face and body in his mind and when he arrived home he searched for a picture of any girl he could imagine to be her. The closest he could find was a cheerleader in a porno but she didn't have those perfect tits or long plump thighs cut by her plaid skirt or little hairs on her cheek that looked like she was sprayed with gold dust in the sunshine.

———

Bobby had enjoyed no release when he killed his Mother. He had just let her go, his actions so practical and steady that even setting her house on fire hadn't given him satisfaction. His urges had been denied so long that they now grew into a low hum of need, constant in his body like a spring was being stretched through his limbs.

A glimpse of the girl was all he wanted each day or all he was allowed because eye contact was forbidden with the tenants, especially for Bobby, whom they had been told had a record. He got by at first by looking at her in a piece of discarded mirror and then used it cleverly he thought, to take pictures and some video on his phone, but this was still dangerous and he refused to jeopardize this job in any way for fear of not seeing her at all. He started to observe her by smell, breathing the perfume mist that lingered outside their apartment door and in their garbage, her garbage in particular, with its cotton balls, Q-tips and other things ripe with the aroma of iron. He knew he could never risk entering the apartment but sometimes ate lunch on the scaffold outside her bedroom looking in at the real-life setting for his increasingly specific ideas.

He tried to be calm as he learned the habits, routines and schedule of what he realized was a small family. The girl's Mother and Father, the Doormen, her friends and even the Construction Foreman seemed to arrange their lives around her presence the way Bobby did. People waited for her or tagged along with her for a block and everyone always paused to watch her walk away. He saw everything like a soap opera in the corner of his eye, the girl's nature becoming clearer even from a distance because the family lived so much of their lives in the street.

Heather, as Bobby now called her in his head after discovering a shiny square envelope from something called the Cystic Fibrosis Foundation addressed to Mrs. Karen Breakstone, was clever with people the way he was, especially her parents; flirting with the baby-faced Father and strong with the heavy-breasted Mother. But he noticed Heather was very different from him at all other times, laughing and confident, kind to her little fat friends, talking only nicely on her phone and even crumbling the remains of her muffin on the sidewalk for the birds. She was radiant with life even when she was alone, or thought she was.

Of course a glimpse of her was never enough and luckily as the days got colder her goose-pimpled legs were often covered in sweatpants that were loose at her waist and one day, as she paused by the awning, they revealed the top of her baby blue panties when she bent over. Bobby saw this from the dumpster by the curb but did not have time to take out his phone. It didn't matter because somehow, as if he had willed it, when Heather ran across the street to join the Father she shot a tiny look back to Bobby and their eyes met for a moment and as all the city sounds fell out of the sky to silence, he tried to remember how to smile.

Bobby now knew everything he needed to know and that his plans were too modest and should go far beyond just locking her in a room and having her in every way from top to bottom in various poses and positions. He was going to have to kill

Heather no matter what to not get caught but he kept thinking about the time he had gone to Catholic church at 13 with a social worker. He remembered that when he took the wafer and the wine he felt them really turn into something in his mouth, like a whiff of smoke from burning cocaine, and after, he ran home on a rampage of bare-handed destruction and knocked over mailboxes and garbage cans and even splintered a car windshield with only his fist. He was sure then that this strength and power were from that tiny part of God he had eaten and he tried for months to take Communion again but the social worker was transferred and Bobby was too shy to enter a church on his own.

That night in his motel room, Bobby lay rigid on the bed staring at her face on his phone, knowing that now that their eyes had met and because she was so precious to all, she would be his wafer and wine. He wondered what kind of white light he might become if he took her in even more ways after he had slowly strangled her. Bobby would have every part of Heather and they would be one inside him and he could be the beginning and ending of everything.

FOUR

SOMETIME BETWEEN HEATHER'S FOURTEENTH birthday and Halloween, Mark got more dire news about his bonus and started looking for another job. He had made the mistake of telling Karen and she was predictably worried but in his corner against the undeserving frat boys who kept surpassing him by playing basketball with the boss and his son. Mark was not a bad prospect; his resumé took credit for the firm's ten-year climb and his years of running had kept him lean and even caused his ample face to finally sit down on his skull, giving him a sober, seasoned look.

———

The interviews started quickly and had to be managed like an affair, with after-hours phone calls and out of the way restaurants so as not to alert the office. Mark would often jog even earlier so that he could meet for breakfast, sometimes in the dark. The emptiness of the city before dawn gave him a chance to rehearse out loud, recalling his victories and experience in broken breaths.

On the day of a particularly promising lead Mark went for an extra-long run and returned to find the water and power had been shut off. As he considered the horror of drying himself with a towel and putting on a suit, he realized the alarm clocks were dead as well and he woke Heather, then Karen, swearing as he slapped on cologne. Karen told him they'd been notified and Mark had little to complain about legitimately and so he silently continued in angry despair on his walk to get two lattes, for Heather and himself. Why were they still in the building, he thought, his neck sweaty against his starched collar, and why did it have to be today and had he put on so much cologne that the woman behind him at the coffee place was sneezing?

He walked back to the apartment with the two coffees sloshing in a tray, recounting his stupidities, including the fact that he would have to drink even more coffee at his interview, and as he was about to cross the street to his apartment, his apartment where Heather was waiting, he froze. Heather was staring at her phone and one of the workers was staring at her. The stare was coming from a short guy in a work apron and was so carnal and intense that Mark charged across the street and pushed Heather away as if he were stepping between her and an oncoming car. Heather was irritated and confused and took her coffee as they started to walk and Mark looked back at the Worker, who had a nearly shaved head of hair, too silver for how young he was, and pale blue eyes, now averted as he went back to shoveling debris.

Mark was so distracted in his interview that he forgot to try and got an actual job offer, but it was no solace as he returned to work, unwrapped his lunch and left for home, anxiety replacing whatever hunger he had. His head swam as he took a post across the street, unsure if he was acting on his desire to spy or for the true security of his daughter who was certainly now just leaving school. He pretended to talk on his phone as the Worker came down to the dumpster with a wheelbarrow and stood casually until, with perfect timing, Heather rounded the corner and he suddenly began to work.

Mark watched as his daughter approached their home, unaware of the long sickening glance she was receiving, and when the creep wiped his mouth, his eyes searching up Heather's skirt as she entered the building, Mark debated yelling across the street or confronting him but instead took a zoomed picture on his phone and somehow found himself in Central Park where he had started his day, his thoughts now unutterable.

He wondered if this short, dirty skinhead was waiting for his daughter not just twice today but on a regular basis and if that shark-eyed look was more than overwhelming lust. It could be the look of a man who had anticipated rejection and hated this willowy young brat who taunted him as she paraded by, possessing everything he could not have. Mark wished it were just desire he had seen directed at his daughter and then he nearly collapsed against a bench to catch his breath, his body having deduced immediately what it took his mind an hour to figure out: the Worker's gaze was so violent and hungry that Mark had actually run away.

★

When Mark came home, Karen was appreciating the hot water and electricity as one does when necessities are restored by fixing dinner, a family meal of tricolored pasta, Heather's favorite. He marched in with his tie down and shirt soaked through and insisted they needed to talk as he went to the bedroom. It wasn't until much later, when Mark sat down to eat, irritated and freshly showered, that Karen realized he had been waiting for her in the bedroom to talk privately. She felt his impatience grow throughout dinner even though it had been pleasant lately since she had learned to make conversation with Heather by casually bringing up debate topics like Radical Islam or Gun Control.

———

By the time Heather's light went out, Mark was halfway through a bottle of whiskey and Karen closed their bedroom door with dread. She remembered the sweat and the shameful look on his face when he had come home and assumed he was about to confess some infidelity or, more likely, that he'd lost his job. She made room for him on the bed but he chose to stand and was emotional as he whispered about the events of his day.

*

Mark hesitated now, not because he was drunk and not because he had drawn a lot of conclusions in such a short time but because he didn't know which details he could share without sounding irrational. He knew better than to show Karen the photo on his phone, so all he could do was explain the danger he'd witnessed and that he had seen that look before in the eyes of one of his Father's star football players and that there were famously two raped dead girls at some southern college to prove it and when he saw Karen actually smile while he was recounting this, he lost his temper. Karen swore that she was relieved not amused that this was the news but she was infuriatingly more concerned about the outcome of his interview than their daughter's peril.

It wasn't up for discussion; either he or Karen, if she thought it more persuasive, would talk to the Foreman in the barest detail and insist that the Worker be let go or at least relocated. This firm statement finally got Karen's attention and she considered but then rejected this option, reminding him that this Worker literally knew where they lived. Mark agreed with her and suggested they go to the police. And say what, exactly? Karen countered, since there was no cause, really, no evidence, no complaint at all other than Mark's feelings, which sounded extreme even to his wife. Mark agreed again and demanded that they move to a hotel tomorrow while they looked for a place to wait out the construction.

Karen calmly reasoned that the exterior work was to be finished by Thanksgiving and it was already Halloween and the idea of relocating this late in the game seemed silly since all the same inconveniences awaited them as two months before. She took his worries seriously but knew that the stress of the apartment and his job search and their personal distance had made him unreasonably fearful. She admitted that she was troubled by those problems as well, not to mention being ignored by her daughter, and frankly she found the workers to be harmless and polite and wasn't even sure which one he was talking about until Mark mentioned that he was white.

Mark swore at her, saying that all of it was bullshit and that the work would take until spring and that they had stayed in the apartment for Heather's well-being, not to make Karen's easy life easier, and she left that fucking kitchen window open all the time so that anyone could catch pneumonia and if it was so hot in there then maybe she should get off her ass and go outside and do something.

Karen was stung. She sure as hell didn't need to defend her life to her own husband and she didn't need to tell him what she did for their family or that she would be fine if he wanted to move out and visit Heather on weekends or that she was staying no matter what and just this week she was going to put out feelers in publishing and how dare he call her selfish when she had an appointment to see a plastic surgeon to make herself more youthful and sexy for him?

But instead of all that, she took a breath and said something she had been thinking for a long time: that Mark's interest in their daughter was unhealthy and made her uncomfortable. She shrouded the accusation in concern but after noting his horrified reaction, retreated slightly from her insinuation and made it worse. She told him bluntly that she didn't know what it was like to be a father and she worried about Heather attracting the wrong types or any types at all, but he was an overprotective mess and pathologically jealous of any man nearby.

Mark was sick at her suggestion and screamed at her hypocrisy. Of all people, she was the one with the obsession. She was the one who couldn't see anything in the world except her daughter. He demanded they move. If she didn't want to do it for him, she should do it for Heather, he yelled, because Karen never did anything for him; he was last on her list and she wouldn't even make him a cup of coffee unless it was to impress Heather.

It felt good for Mark to say this but he wished he could take it back when she grabbed a pillow and left the room. As he sat alone on their unmade bed, his anger turned inward because he knew he deserved all of this for gutlessly sharing real danger with his wife. He now understood that this was an emergency and not an excuse for the truth to come out between them. Karen's terrible words were clearly her envy out to destroy his closeness with Heather and he just had to be bigger and stronger now. He apologized to Karen with no caveats and agreed that he was overreacting and that they were not going to move.

Karen slipped into bed next to Mark, full of false forgiveness. In her mind, nothing had been resolved and she felt no regret for what she thought, only that she'd said it out loud. She stole a look at him over the top of her tablet as he turned in his sleep and couldn't believe the funny, adoring man she had married had become a paranoid failure who didn't even see her. She turned off the light and thought of the future and imagined having a lover, maybe one of the handsome fathers at the school who was just looking for a fling, and she dozed off with her hand resting inertly on her sex, soothing herself the way she did when she was a child.

Mark pretended to sleep while he considered if he should warn Heather or even tell her but his hold on her affection was so tenuous he dared not disturb it. He thought it wouldn't be kidnapping if he took his own child to Turks and Caicos for a perfect vacation and then maybe Karen would get the message and join them. He was so sorry he had told her. He should have surprised them all with a sudden vacation and paid someone to move them before they returned but now it was too late and he thought about how he should take Heather away anywhere and how he could drop something heavy from high up like a plumber's wrench or a brick and crush the Worker's skull.

*

Heather read in the dark on her phone as she did most nights, aware that her parents were coiled with the tension of not being themselves while they thought she was awake. She heard their bickering that night but had learned to ignore it years ago because it was always about her and never going to go anywhere serious. Her Mother and Father were especially blind to feelings. Her Father denied he even had feelings and her Mother assumed everyone shared hers. Heather didn't know for years that her ability to see people's feelings and even feel them sometimes was unusual and when she discovered that the cruelty and rudeness that adults and friends inflicted on each other was unintentional or at least uninformed, she decided to withdraw, overwhelmed by the pain of typical human behavior.

Heather had always felt beautiful and sensed what was fair and known that everyone wanted to try their best but seeing how different her parents were at home and how they couldn't share in each other's happiness made her question what she had done to their lives. She used to listen to their fights, sometimes even sneaking into their room to hide at the foot of their bed and pray for them to divorce so that her love would finally be divided equally between them and she could smile at the world without worrying that Mark or Karen would intercept it.

As Heather read about the world's events, her heart would hurt but she was always looking for a new angle to build a debate case that would send her to the Stanford Invitational in January, which meant a trip to California and a shot at the nationals if her Father didn't stop it. She loved arguing and traveling and meeting new kids but she chose debate with its path to public policy and the law, having gradually learned that neither of her parents were satisfied with their meaningless careers. She swore that she would do everything to avoid their unhappiness by studying hard and trying to make friends and not enemies. She also loved winning, which she did often and politely, appearing earnestly concerned with facts and morality but secretly cheering with victory.

This dishonesty troubled her, as did her increasing interest in herself. It had been years since she'd worried about her Father having a heart attack while jogging or her Mother being wrecked with sadness when she left for school. But why should she care about them? Didn't both of her parents deserve to be ignored for being exhaustingly needy of her time and affection? Hadn't they earned it? Other parents acted similarly but Heather's were the most suffocating and although it took some effort, she was never disloyal by sharing their behavior, knowing it would be a catastrophic betrayal if the world discovered the Breakstone family wasn't perfect.

The more difficult secret, which the world must never see, was the melancholy that lived just under her smile. Heather knew she should give it up or replace it with gratitude and she would gladly give it up if only it didn't feel so good to be sad. Her favorite moment each day was right after she put her phone on the dresser and before she fell asleep, when she listened to the traffic and thought about each lonely horn, so random, and all the adults and the places they were going and how they were in such a rush.

———

Heather wanted to write so many thoughts down but she knew a diary was beyond the amount of privacy her Mother would tolerate and so much stayed inside or came out in whispers when she sat in front of the mirror on the back of her bedroom door. Between the books her Mother gave her and countless classes at school, she was embarrassed yet prepared for the hormonal on-slaught ahead and she was always taking note of it. She thought her hair could use some lightening and one of her teeth was turned and she was still too young to know for sure but it looked like she was going to have clear skin and that was a gift.

She joined the other girls in their complaints about their weight or uneven breasts but she had become increasingly aware that her tall, long-legged, narrow-waisted, and for now nearly C-cup figure was rare, if not ideal, and she was beginning to sense everything that meant when she looked in magazines or walked down the street or got a stare from one of the building's construction workers when she came and went.

———

She realized now that her friends wanted to be seen and pretending to be a bad girl was the best way for them to both defy their parents and get a certain kind of attention. She wasn't sure how much interest she could stand and only went along with her girlfriends to not get caught being a baby or incur more envy by adding purity to their list of her perfections. So, like them, she started to use every moment out of her parents' sight, whether walking to and from school or in Central Park or even hiding on the roof of their building, to talk loud on her phone and smoke cigarettes and chew gum and wear makeup and more revealing clothing, including temporary alterations to her school uniform like rolling her skirt waist to raise the hemline and stealing smaller blouses from the lost-and-found to accentuate her bust. She even borrowed the fantasies of her friends about the girl-faced boys who sang the music they liked and the vague scenarios of being whisked away and embraced in the dark and was, like them, open to the idea of being kissed passionately but truly scared and not ready for anything else.

———

Heather hated that she couldn't talk to her Mother anymore and couldn't figure out how it had become so awkward, but it had and she was sickened by her Mother's phony lightness as she clumsily begged for intimacy. She could feel her Mother's desperation for any detail related to Heather's sexual stirrings so she could cry and share and urge control with embarrassing condescension.

Heather refused to touch on the subject even though she knew her Mother would be put at ease knowing that being at a girls' school meant only a few girls were having sex and all the boys that Heather met were either shy like her or interested in those few girls having sex. She would never tell her Mother any of that because it would only open the conversation to the more troubling monologue in Heather's head, which was her growing disgust with who they were and how much they had.

Their zip code was almost number one on the list

of the wealthiest in the country and her Father didn't make anything and her Mother didn't do anything and their apartment wasn't gigantic but it was unnecessarily lavish and velvet and they used too much and threw away too much and, worst of all, didn't care. How many tropical islands could they visit and still ignore the rampant poverty just over the resort fence? Her parents weren't bad people but they were living in a self-righteous delusion that they deserved everything they had.

She had tried to alert both of them separately to the injustice of their position but neither would fight and they individually referred to her, as if rehearsed, as their most prized possession: the thing that money could not buy. She knew what her parents meant by this, the love they were expressing, but she also knew they were poisoned with some disease of wealth that had turned them into half-people with coffee machines and cash registers where their hearts should be.

Heather knew she was infected by this too and fought to control her gnawing need to shop and spend and get a treat for doing ordinary things. And so it was that by the time most people moved out of the building and the trucks came, she had resolved to overcome her powerful impulse towards comfort and luxury and accept all the inconveniences of construction as payment due on their unearned life. She even resisted being a brat and didn't join in the daily though well-founded complaints of her Father, which was difficult for her since it was so annoying to be checked out all the time by that Worker at her own front door.

It was too embarrassing to tell her Father anyway and she knew her Mother was oblivious as usual because once when they were looking for a package and the Doorman was gone, Heather had suggested that they ask the Worker out front and her Mother had no idea who she was talking about. Heather clarified that he was the only white one and even though his silvery hair was cut so short he looked bald, he wasn't and had the smooth skin, strong jaw, and clear blue eyes of a young man.

———

She couldn't tell her Mother that she wondered about him more every day, where he was from and what he was like and how could it be that he was the handsome one and was doing ten-hour shifts for the last two months to renovate their mansion and her Mother didn't even see him? Maybe, Heather thought, her Mother would have remembered him if he had looked at her the way he looked at Heather, especially the one or two times their eyes had met and she'd felt as if she were naked in the street.

No doubt it would have bothered her Mother as it did Heather at first. It had annoyed and then outraged her, making her think of all the entitlements of men and how they didn't have the right to just look at women and disrupt them that way. But he was only looking at her, wasn't he, and had never looked at her Mother and over time Heather knew he saw all of her somehow.

He was out there every day as far as she knew and she couldn't tell her Mother that she wondered on the few days he wasn't if he had forgotten about her. She couldn't explain that it didn't bother her at all anymore and that most nights she thought about their slight interactions and imagined him or her sense of him and realized that his looking at her, and even more his trying not to look at her, gave her a warm ache in her stomach that moved all the way down.

She wanted to talk to him. She wanted to tell him that she wasn't like her mother, that she saw all people and knew that he was horribly forced to behave like a servant. She wouldn't condescend to him like some spoiled private school heiress who got to live there with everything. She could only guess at the deprivation and circumstances that brought someone to that point in their life and she wondered if he was intelligent and what his voice sounded like and if she could ever do anything for those who lacked. She could never tell her mother that she would be whole one day because she would act with her heart and give everything away, including herself if necessary, so that someone could benefit from their years of effortless accumulation. What she really wanted to do was tell the Worker that she saw him.

"Is my Mother home yet?"

Bobby heard the voice and knew who it was and couldn't believe she was so close. He looked up, unable to answer, and saw the wind blow her hair into her mouth and watched her pull it away from her full lips with one perfectly bent finger. He finally managed to say, "Not yet," and probably stared too long before remembering he should make a smile for her, but she took it and smiled back and walked inside after a moment with her skirt bouncing high against her ass.

Bobby relived every second of their interaction that night. It had so many parts and they had both behaved even better than he hoped they would, with her not just talking to him but inviting him as a co-conspirator in her plan to do something bad while her Mother was away. He tried not to spin the event any further but his imagination took him to her bedroom where she had invited him and he could see himself pushing into her and feel she was like his Mother's kimono inside.

A week earlier it had been Halloween and Bobby knew that he could not wear a mask but he liked it when adults did and hid their dumb faces and he especially liked Heather dressed up like a kitten, a black dot on the end of her nose like she'd leaned into a screen door. He stood up as she walked towards him that day because his back was hurting from working hard enough to never lose his job. Still, his body was calm and his muscles relaxed naturally when he saw her. It was possible, he thought, that they were getting used to each other. He decided that day as she walked by all in black that there was only one real test and that was for her to speak to him and prove herself worthy by stepping away from her world and begging to be in his.

And now that she had actually spoken to him, he was so happy and surprised and harder than ever. He had been hoping to will it or compel her but as she spoke, she seemed under her own power, not his. Heather was something different for sure, something even more than he could understand before. Was it possible now that consuming her was something less than he wanted? Her death in his hands would be exquisite and Bobby had thought it was both their destinies but he suddenly saw it for what it was: temporary. All of the pictures in his mind changed and he now wanted her to come to him on her own and he could barely wait until the next morning to see her as it was, so what would happen if she were truly gone?

FIVE

THE BREAKSTONES' STREET WAS clogged with traffic at all hours due to the construction, which, along with the mounting garbage bags and falling leaves, provided cover for Mark for those tense minutes the next day when Heather came and went. He didn't know what he was doing there exactly other than being at the ready to come to Heather's aid and of course to get some kind of proof, not to throw in Karen's face but to share with the police. He knew he had to do something when he saw his daughter and the Worker twice that day, sliding by each other silently like figurines on a medieval clock.

———

Karen had remained in a pout and Mark knew to be sweet and apologetic as if he had drunk too much at a party. She was unaware as they went to bed that night that Mark saw himself loosening the scaffold or cutting the 220-volt wiring in the wet basement or, the most intriguing, luring the Worker up to their apartment and shooting him because he had been harassing his daughter, ask anyone, and had broken in with a kitchen knife, which Mark would place in his hand after the fact. Mark was able to sleep finally, but only when lulled by repeated scenes of the Worker's death, usually by choking him with bare hands.

After a few days Mark confided to his assistant that he was job hunting and asked her to help hide his strange schedule. He had started to watch his own apartment building for two hours twice a day and saw that the Worker's ritual encounters were sloppy and obvious to all except his daughter and that the construction crew seemed as wary of him as Mark. They commuted together, packed in rusty pickups with Jersey license plates, but always made the

Worker crouch in the truck bed. They socialized and laughed a few times a day with coffee and cigarettes, except for the Worker, who was rarely in the penthouse where most of the work happened and who had all the worst jobs and wasn't even invited to lunch.

The intensity of Mark's surveillance didn't waver, fueled by both his need to protect Heather and his fear of being seen. He knew he should at least rehearse an excuse if Karen or Heather or a neighbor or these people on their street, the tourists, nannies, deliverymen, school kids and women in yoga pants, possibly saw him. But they didn't see him and Mark's vigilance was rewarded that day when, on her return from school, he saw Heather speak with the Worker.

Heather had initiated the exchange and it was brief and seemed as stunning to the Worker as it did to Mark. It didn't matter what the two had talked about, or if they already knew each other, or how shy the Worker's response was. All that mattered to Mark was that his daughter had stuck her innocent hand into this flame with a friendly smile and that the Worker hadn't seen Mark at all.

The only thing that stifled a complete panic was Mark's gut sensation that opportunity had declared itself. His calculations were instant. Here was an aging, unskilled, and probably uneducated day laborer, barely hanging on to the fringe of society, without a union or money or any protection in what was an extremely hazardous workplace. It got colder and grayer as Mark watched Heather eventually go into the building and he waited, shivering for another two hours until the crew knocked off and the Worker got in the truck.

Mark thought about going to an Internet café so that he could research where to buy a gun without leaving an electronic trail on his phone or computers, but he thought when was the last time he'd seen an Internet café and decided he would just go to the library first thing in the morning. He figured that the only practical idea was to hire a private guard like the billionaires did, to watch and protect his family.

When he finally went in, Mark hugged Heather and smiled at Karen and thought he would ask his boss to recommend a reliable, discreet security company. He went to bed thinking he would do that in the morning although he knew now he did not want to seek anyone's help, in fact, he did not want questions of any kind and he fell asleep easily that night, exhausted at having reached a resolution.

Mark's dreams that night were so vivid, he wasn't sure if he was asleep. He would see himself climbing the outside of their building, using the ladder of the scaffolding and he would look out over the neighborhood towards the treetops of the park, then the other direction, a spire of a church and Park Avenue, a yellow blur of taxis. Then, after that, he would peer into Heather's bedroom. She was gone so he would look into his own bedroom window and see Heather on their bed facing the ceiling in only socks, cut open like a deer, bloodless on their white chenille duvet.

———

This was strangely not horrific to him and he found himself in the room at the foot of the bed as her mutilated corpse spoke to him, her face alive and normal. She said something like "Daddy, why did you do this to me?" That was exactly what she said, and on what seemed like the third repetition of this dream, he knew it was a dream and woke himself from it, anticipating that perhaps he might never want to sleep again.

Mark did not believe in the supernatural or in giving any prophetic qualities to dreams. He knew this image was merely an expression of what was on his waking mind and the interpretation was hardly complex. He knew it meant that he was afraid for Heather's life and should something happen to her, even she would know he was responsible. As he sat in the hallway outside the door of his daughter's room, trying to strike her ghostly accusations from his mind, he became aware that the dream might have another meaning. What if Karen had been right? What if his mind had been overrun with the irrational? What had he really seen except another man, and God there were so many who wanted his daughter?

He refused to believe the disgusting things Karen had suggested but maybe she had put the thought in his mind and maybe he had gotten carried away and maybe that dream had happened because in the past few days there were no other thoughts allowed. He wasn't abnormal, he knew that. He wasn't jealous of those men, not in that way, and he couldn't imagine someone penetrating his daughter but he certainly didn't want to be her lover in place of them. He only wanted her to be his daughter the way she was now and never stop. Mark understood he had to let go of Heather and let her grow up and that he had to accept whatever their relationship became because that's what parents did. He knew that it would break his heart and that was normal.

*

Karen could not shake the big argument with Mark. She felt guilty at first, knowing that she had started things with her insecure guesses at his thoughts and she had merely been defending that stupid mistake when she lashed out. He hadn't lost his job. He wasn't having an affair. It was only a misunderstanding between them and she was really kicking herself for not keeping her feelings to herself under any attack, yet he seemed so crazed and in the end maybe he needed an excuse to express his real feelings too. It was cruel, what Mark had said, but it confirmed her belief that he saw absolutely no value in what she did. But it was also good, what Mark said, because after years of being appreciated less and less, she was awakened to the fact that she should do more for herself.

She also needed more people in her life. Being mostly with strangers had kept her in her head too much and she was frequently anxious and scattered. She had always wanted close friendships but now she saw that her whole life, some sense of competition had brought out people's worst behavior and most social interactions were shallow and boastful on all sides. Karen hoped that finding a confidante would be possible now that the ladies were all equally humbled by their rebellious teens, sexless marriages, food obsessions and real estate woes.

———

The day after the big fight with Mark, Karen remembered a mother at the school who had disappeared when her daughter had chosen the diving team over debate. Karen had always liked her, and she had always been friendly with funny stories she got from her husband, a high-profile divorce attorney. Karen called under the guise of a possible shared fundraiser to cover travel expenses for the underprivileged girls in their daughters' respective activities. She was nervous as she dialed and made up a name for the nonexistent event, her professional mind awake after all these years, rejecting puns on "splash" and "resolution" before arriving at "The Competitors, a Celebration!" They had lunch that day and neither shared much but Karen enjoyed being one of those people who talked about movie stars and celebrities, especially their private or romantic lives, with judgment and disgust.

The day after that, Karen got a job at a hospital thrift shop on Second Avenue, as a volunteer of course, but five hours, five days a week, and she had a key to the front door. The benefits of working

MATTHEW WEINER

were immediate because the rest of the all-female
staff, many of them cancer survivors, were older or
looked older, so that men who came in, usually to
buy a Burberry, angled for Karen's attention and
flirted the minute their wives weren't looking. The
store benefited as well, since Karen became their
biggest patron after two days, indulging her long-
trained eye for luxury, especially the used couture
fashions for which her relative youth and exercised
body made her the sole customer.

Karen left the clothes, plus the jewelry and lug-
gage she'd acquired, in the back of the store and
tried them on during her breaks, considering if
they needed tailoring and when she could wear
them and how well a suitcase went with her new,
old look. In this ritual, she suddenly appreciated
her privacy, wondering why she had done so little
for herself for so long and knowing that Mark
had no idea how lucky he was. She was thin and
viable and just as glaringly mismatched to his ug-
liness as the day they'd met.

Barely a week had passed since Mark had yelled
at her and his attempts to apologize were no more

convincing than his recent kindness. Heather might have bought his sunny smile but Karen could see the cracks in the corners of his mouth and the dark circles around his eyes that revealed his frustration. She lay awake in bed that night and felt for him and how small he'd become as he marshaled his waning potency against imagined enemies.

She might just do that fundraiser and Heather's sense of charity might be piqued enough to chair the student committee. Karen was so pleased that her friend, soon to be one of many, thought it was genuine genius and that they should have dinner and plan it with her husband, the divorce attorney, who could be helpful in so many ways. While Karen smiled to herself in the dark, Mark woke with a start, sweaty and afraid, and she rolled over without sympathy, certain he was suddenly aware that she was strong and getting stronger; her mind sharpening on its own, coming up with ideas without effort, big ideas.

★

The next morning Mark showered and went to work, glad that he had a routine and happy to do his job, especially since he was exhausted and had to fight off moments of nausea every time that horrible dream flashed in his mind. He needed to run but didn't have the energy. Everything had been on his mind; the Worker, Heather's face, and of course Karen's judgment, and he now considered that he was deliberately thinking about these things to avoid the real crisis. It was true that his job was in flux and his apartment being renovated but his discontent preceded these events and he looked out his window to the Manhattan skyline littered with skeletal steel and cranes and took in its loneliness. One day Karen had just stopped laughing at his jokes and noticing him at all and Heather had become his audience.

Mark sat there, sipping watery office coffee, wondering what else there would be in life after raising this child. Had he sacrificed his happiness for theirs? Willingly of course, but he and Karen were now far apart and most men would be thinking about a clean start with half their money and another woman. Heather had witnessed their misery and was old enough to understand a divorce would be for the best. Still, despite all the machinery of civilization devoted to splitting up and moving on, Mark couldn't imagine the strength needed to actually do such a thing.

His Father, the football coach, had been a physical man and ever since Mark had flinched the first time he heard the grunt of a tackle during a scrimmage, his Father had regarded him as afraid. Of course he was afraid. His Father's forearms were huge and his temper capricious and he took defeat very seriously in all aspects of his life so Mark learned to take a beating and try to correct his behavior to avoid such one-sided confrontations. Mark needed to run, and not in a loop, not from home and back but from home in one direction until he couldn't run anymore and was too tired to do anything but start over wherever he was.

Just before lunch, Mark decided to go home and get his running clothes and after he put on his coat, he erased the picture of the Worker on his phone. It disgusted him and made him angry and although he enjoyed the brief satisfaction of what was an intentionally symbolic act, he wondered if one could truly erase anything these days.

———

Stepping outside the building into the gray noon light he was calm, hailing a cab and feeling a tingle in his nose of what smelled like the first wintry day. He thought about Heather and how if she had been a son, none of these feelings would exist. He also admitted to himself that she would be terribly damaged if her parents divorced and that he had been filled with irrational emotions lately from skipping both sleep and exercise.

The years to come would probably go as planned with him and Karen together until, assuming neither of them exceeded their expected lifespan, someone would be alone. From someone's old age, he saw that Heather had a remarkable life as a lawyer or even the president and that thanks to him she wouldn't end up like his poor Sister, the perfectionist of starvation, who never got to know what promise lay beyond that feat.

When Mark got out of the cab he was relieved that the construction crew was at lunch but as he walked through the lobby to the elevator he noticed the Doorman was gone as well and the Worker was sitting on the radiator box looking at his phone and drinking what Mark assumed was liquor, from a paper bag. Mark waited for the elevator, his resolve to ignore everything undone by the hairs rising on his neck. He turned in time to catch the Worker staring at him.

Their connection was brief but total and Mark felt his guts push down as if he was going to shit right where he stood. It was unmistakable now that an animal was in their lobby; eyes heavy-lidded with indifferent hunger, shoulders arched and taut, ready to pounce. Mark's heart thudded as he considered how long this thing would be on his doorstep, unsatisfied with anything but his child.

When the elevator opened Mark should have gone upstairs, changed into his running clothes and left, but instead he held the door with his forearm. His mouth was almost too dry to speak and he hoped he wouldn't sound scared as he asked the Worker if everyone was at lunch. He couldn't believe he had spoken, his voice so loud, every guilty syllable slapping off the marble walls. The Worker nodded yes, and Mark understood his mind had been far ahead that morning when he had erased that photo. In fact, it was probably hours ago even that he had decided what had to be done, readied himself for an opportunity, and begun covering it up.

*

"Could you help me move something upstairs?" Heather's Dad asked. Bobby had his back up a little when her Father stomped in more bitchy and annoyed than usual and, since the crew wasn't supposed to eat in the lobby or certainly have a beer, Bobby thought the old man might give him hell or rat him out to the Foreman. Bobby had never even taken a good look at him; he wasn't interesting, and when he was with Heather, he was just in the way, circling her like a bothersome fly. Now up close, he was exactly what Bobby expected, one of those douchebags who thought the whole world worked for him and despite his king-in-his-castle voice, he was just a fat-faced punk and scaredy cat, especially today without his fancy briefcase.

None of this kept Bobby from the pleasure of anticipating how he could soon be inside Heather's house and so he trotted to the elevator, putting his head down to hide his eagerness. In the foyer, Heather's Dad rushed to their front door but couldn't find the key right away and checked over his shoulder so much that Bobby thought he needed help. The front door finally opened and a wall of heat wafted out so rich with all of Heather's smells, that Bobby had to steady himself in the doorway.

He followed Heather's Dad through the stifling entry past the lush living room and into a narrow hallway where Bobby knew the bedrooms were. He checked for any sign of her, a shoe, a sweater, and was tempted to veer off or just choke her old man out and be ready in her bedroom when she came home. But he just followed, half listening to her bragging Father, who was now in a sweat and led them towards the kitchen where the outside air was coming in from the open window.

Bobby had seen many apartments this nice but
only from a scaffolding and had never been inside
one that wasn't demolished or under construction. It would have seemed bigger without so
much stuff in it; still, he was thrilled with the
white walls and green carpet and all the TVs and
brass trinkets and he wanted to sit in the stuffed
red furniture and have a whiskey from that crystal
glass. He knew that these were the people that
went to the movies all the time and ate in restaurants and flew on planes and had pictures of
horses on everything.

He looked at her Father's back and thought the
poor guy probably wasn't that bad; he had a wife
with big tits and together the two of them had
made Heather. In fact, these people had made all
of this and whether they liked it or not, they'd
made it all for him.

Bobby walked into the kitchen where the cabinets
and even the refrigerator had glass doors and were
packed with food, and tried to imagine a way this

could all work out. For the first time he thought far beyond killing her. He saw her at the stovetop in a baby blue bathrobe, frying him an egg.

★

By the time Mark was at the front door, he regretted talking to the Worker at all. The two men had been so close in the elevator that Mark gagged on the stink of beer and cigarettes and dirty clothes and could clearly see a pulse throbbing under the shaved silver hair of his temples. He watched as the Worker leaned on the front door after closing it, taking a deep breath through his nose as if to inhale the whole place. Mark didn't want to turn his back on him but couldn't risk catching those eyes and revealing his fear and he found himself backing away from the Worker while yammering like a real estate agent about the various spaces that made up their apartment.

Mark had imagined killing him many times but now in reality he had no gun, no big wrench, and certainly no physical advantage. He could never get his hands around that thick neck. He felt a chill in his spine as he realized he had done nothing more than invite the danger into his home where he could die at the hands of this short, hunched simian who still hadn't said a word.

Mark had to keep walking, and he inventoried every weapon they passed, the crockery umbrella stand, then the fireplace poker or that mahogany humidor; they were heading towards the kitchen. There were knives in there. If he could get to the kitchen first he could grab the chef's knife and turn and surprise him. Or better, make a break for the door and run down the steps to the street.

Mark sped up as he heard the heavy boots a few steps behind him but then just watched as the Worker passed by and landed in the open space of the kitchen, facing him. Mark's heart sank and raced at the same time. The Worker was six feet away and out of reach, a hulking silhouette against the bright gray light from the window behind him.

Bobby looked around the kitchen but now saw nothing, his mind and body too occupied with the future. He could never go back to school but was good at saving money and he could get Heather a house, no, a home. She was born rich, so her parents would never want to see her go without and so they would help them out, and happily, because Bobby would be working his hardest and everyone respected that. And he would come up behind her as she cooked and wrap his arms around her waist and she would smile back at him, the way he'd seen lovers do on TV.

The Worker's face was dark except for his blue eyes as he took a step towards the stove. Mark felt his quadriceps tighten as he lowered to a tackling stance and drove with his full weight into the Worker's hips, pushing him backwards into the low open window, and Bobby, off balance, folded easily through and fell the ten stories without even a scream, the wet thud of his body coinciding with a car horn.

*

That day Karen had arranged lunch with an old friend from her publicity days who was now the executive secretary to an editor in chief of a women's magazine. Karen wanted to share her rekindled ambitions but they mostly reminisced and while this friend hadn't eclipsed Karen, she had many stories of their past underlings who now ran the world of media. Karen remembered why they'd lost touch as her friend made it clear there was no place for Karen in the publishing world and perhaps there never was and that she was best suited for the unpaid-mother work of charities and thrift shops.

As she walked into the apartment, she felt years of regret in her stomach and a wave of warmth that could have been the onset of menopause and she plodded through the heat of the entry towards the cool air of the kitchen. Mark sat at the table in a T-shirt, his head down on his folded arms, the wide-open window blowing icy cold at his back. She called his name and he looked up with sickness, his face wrinkled and older than she remembered from this morning, if she had even looked at him this morning.

Seeing that his weakness demanded her comfort, she crouched next to him and he told her in a low but steady voice that he had pushed the Worker out the window and that he was dead in the space between the buildings. Karen rushed to the window and looked down to see Bobby's body, a pool of blood under his head, one of his legs bent impossibly backwards so that his foot was beneath his shoulder.

She sat down next to Mark as he stumbled through a clear confession that was incriminating in every detail and as she listened, she became aware that he had ruined their lives and she slapped his face with full force. Mark didn't react, but took her hands one at a time and looked her in the eye. "I know in my heart. I am certain." He said, "Whatever problems this family has, there is no family without her."

She heard him and took in the whole room for a moment and saw from some bird's-eye view that they were small and alone. She knew he was not able to think right now and the whole apartment was asking her what to do and she finally burst into tears, her hands loose in her lap.

Mark stared as she caught her breath and then she sternly addressed him, wiping her eyes, suggesting they pick Heather up at debate practice and have dinner out and come home late enough to act surprised with whatever happened. Mark looked down again and nodded and she then stood and went to the espresso machine and in those next minutes there was silence except for the clink of china and the hiss of steam as Karen prepared a cappuccino and placed it before her husband and watched him sip it as if it were medicine.

*

When the Breakstone family returned to the apartment some hours later, Karen expected that the street would be lit by police cars and the building surrounded by crime tape and she would have to do her best to shake Mark out of his daze and into an attitude of shock as they pushed past onlookers into the building. The officer on the scene would have little information and an investigation was pending and everyone should go back to their apartments and try to process that there had been an accident and this happened sometimes and luckily they were all okay. Karen would then suggest they stay in a hotel for the night and finally rouse Mark to agree and leave, his arm around their daughter in comfort as her backpack hung from her limp hand and dragged on the dusty marble.

But the building was dark when they came home, never more quiet and seemingly abandoned, so they simply headed upstairs and went to sleep. Mark went first since he'd had many drinks and no food at the bistro where they had spontaneously celebrated how Heather had been promoted to varsity debate even though she was a freshman. Karen watched for Heather's light to go out and then undressed and got into bed without brushing her teeth, resisting the urge to look and see if the Worker's body was still there.

She stared at Mark while he slept so deeply, her worry sitting in her belly like a cramp. She realized that in the days to come and perhaps long into the future, it would be her responsibility to keep him from any compulsion to confess. She would have to stand between his guilt and whatever ghost was rising from the alley at that very moment.

In their dark bedroom, Karen looked at him and knew that he must have had his reasons because she knew him and could never be afraid of him and she was suddenly released from all anxiety because she knew now they were bound together forever. She touched him until he stirred and then made love to him and was aggressive and on top and he was drunk enough to forget everything he was and respond with the force of fresh desire.

Bobby's body was not discovered until the next morning when his replacement on the crew was relieving himself in the alley, and the newspapers, then the coroner, ruled his death a work-related accident. Heather was touched by the tragedy and marked the spot with flowers and Mark and Karen waited a full month before putting their apartment on the market.

ACKNOWLEDGMENTS

Writing this book has been a life-changing experience and a childhood dream realized, and like everything I've ever done, I could not have done it alone. These thank-yous come in the order in which the encouragement and support was received.

First, thank you to A. M. Homes, who was generous enough not only to share her writing but to sense my anxiety at the change in my writing life and suggest, then make it possible, for me to spend time at Yaddo. None of this would have happened without her.

I owe so much to the spirit, energy and intelligence of the Yaddo residents in the fall of 2015, including Eric Lane, Patricia Volk, James Godwin, Christopher Robinson, Lisa Endriss, Nate Heiges, Gavin Kovite, Rachel Eliza Griffiths, Pilar Gallego, and especially Isabel Fonseca and Matt Taber who heard as many versions of the story as the trees did and pushed me just hard enough.

Thank you to Semi Chellas for slogging

through the first draft and showing me how to use blank space. She is a writer's writer and makes everyone less afraid.

Thank you to some other early readers who really filled my sails on an unsteady ship: Ann Weiss, Richard LaGravenese, Bryan Lourd, John Campisi, Jeanne Newman, David Chase, Blake McCormick, Karen Brooks Hopkins, Amanda Wolf, Gabrielle Altheim, Molly Hermann, Joshua Oppenheimer, James L. Brooks, Jessica Paré, Sarena Cohen, Madeline Low, Erin Levy, Gianna Sobol, Abby Grossberg, Lydia Dubois-Wetherwax, Christopher Noxon, Milton Glaser, Lisa Klein, David O. Russell, Lisa Albert, Jack Dishel, Regina Spektor, Sydney Miller, Michele Robertson, and my parents, Leslie and Judith Weiner.

Thank you to Alana Newhouse for seeing the value in something so strange. She is a champion, a believer and forever my comrade.

To my agent Jin Auh, for her unflagging confidence in me and her fierceness towards all others. Also to Andrew Wylie and Luke Ingram, of the Wylie Agency.

To my editor and ally Judy Clain, whose remarkable smarts with both words and people have won my trust for life. She made this book better and kept me from making it worse. To Reagan Arthur and the incredible team at Little, Brown and Company: Lucy Kim, Mario Pulice, Craig Young, Nicole Dewey, Jayne Yaffe Kemp, Mary Tondorf-Dick, and Alexandra Hoopes.

To Francis Bickmore, my editor at Canongate, whose guidance and care were essential.

To Jenna Frazier, my writing assistant, whose insight, skill, perfectionism, and taste guided me daily through the whole process.

So many people helped me become a writer not only by taking me seriously, but by making me take myself less seriously. There are teachers, mentors, colleagues and most importantly other writers who have challenged me, scolded me, and answered my dumb questions. They are too numerous to name, but Jeremy Mindich has been the most consistent and loving friend that anyone could ever want.

Okay, this is coming last on the page, but only because it supersedes everything else. To my sons, Marten, Charlie, Arlo and Ellis. You make me laugh, you make me cry, you make me not want to go to work, and I can't get over how much I learn from you. I hope to be like you when I grow up.

And to Linda Brettler, my love and the truest artist I've ever known. How could I have been so lucky?